Old Jake's Skirts

Old Jake's Skirts

by C. ANNE SCOTT

illustrated by
DAVID SLONIM

rising moon
Books for Young Readers from Northland Publishing

DAVID SLONIM WOULD LIKE TO THANK *Bonnie Slonim and Dan Wright for vital support through every stage of this project; Lee Griffith for wise counsel; C. W. Mundy for "chutzpah" in painting; Dan Gerhartz for sensitivity in painting; Bob Farlow for solid critiques and a great old trunk; the models, Forrest "Sonny" Smith (Old Jake), Bob Farlow (Old Jake #2), Mike Badgley (Eb Sweeney), Wanda Henson (Rosie), Elva Mae Hamilton, Thelma M. Carpenter, Bess Newman, and Sue Harvey (Ladies' Committee), Rebekah Gray (Sarah), Mike Gray (Otis Brown), Gentle Ben of Fia Whirlwind Bloodhounds, Summitville, Indiana (Shoestring); and thanks to Mrs. Henderson of Dewey, Arizona, for graciously allowing me to photograph and paint her farm. Special thanks to Rudy Ramos, Erin Murphy, David Jenney, & co. at Northland Publishing for making this possible. Psalm 115:1.*

C. ANNE SCOTT *would like to offer thanks to Erin Murphy and her compadres at Northland for loving this story; to David Slonim for his sensitive insights and enthusiasm, and for rescuing it artistically; to my son Ben for his valuable suggestions; to the Scribblers of Amarillo, you know why; and finally to Dian Curtis Regan, beloved mentor.*

The illustrations were rendered in oil paint
The type was set in Janson
Composed in the United States of America
Art Directed by Rudy J. Ramos
Designed by Billie Jo Bishop
Edited by Stephanie Bucholz
Production Supervised by Lisa Brownfield

Printed in Hong Kong by Wing King Tong Co., Ltd.

FIRST IMPRESSION, March 1998
Second Printing, February 1999
ISBN 0-87358-615-8

Library of Congress Catalog Card Number 97-42328
Cataloging-in-Publication Data
Scott, C. Anne.
Old Jake's skirts / by C. Scott : illustrated by David Slonim.
p.   cm.
Summary: A reclusive pumpkin farmer finds an abandoned steamer
trunk filled with cotton calico skirts which he eventually uses
around the house in ways which seem to bring him luck.
ISBN 0-87358-615-8 (hc)
[1. Skirts—Fiction. 2. Farm life—Fiction. 3. Lost and found
possessions—Fiction.] I. Slonim, David, ill. II. Title.
PZ7.S416801 1998
[Fic]—dc21   97-42328

0771/5M/2-99

For Benjamin, Prince among sons.

—C. A. S.

For Bonnie, "as gentle as them skirts."

—D. S.

OLD JAKE GROUND HIS BEAT-UP TRUCK TO A STOP, unwired the coat hanger holding the door shut, and eased out of his seat. His hound dog bailed out of the back, ran up front, and circled the old steamer trunk in the road as if it were a trapped jackrabbit.

"Whatcha reckon it is, Shoestring?"

Old Jake's headlights had picked out the form of the trunk a few yards back. It was still dawn: He had wanted an early start to town to pick up supplies at the general store. Now this trunk was in his way.

Shoestring sniffed at its base and barked. "Be still, dog," Jake said. "A little ol' trunk can't hurt nuthin'." Shoestring slunk away from the trunk and sat down beside him. Old Jake reached down and absentmindedly scratched his hound's head as he puzzled about what to do.

"Musta fallen off some poor feller's pickup. Best we take it on to town," he muttered as he slowly hunched over to lift it. A bone or two popped in his back. "Hope it ain't books," he said. But when Old Jake got the trunk airborne, he found it was actually light. " 'Tain't books, Shoestring. Could be feathers."

He shoved it into the back of his truck, slammed the tailgate shut, and traveled the last few miles to town.

"Mercy, Jake. What you been feedin' Shoestring? That dog's grown near ten foot since I seen him last."

"Ain't grown none," Old Jake replied in a gravelly voice.

Old Jake was Eb Sweeney's first customer that morning. He always liked to get to Eb's first, buy his things, and clear out before the town talkers arrived for their morning round of gossip. He stepped beside the storekeeper and, sure enough, from the window it appeared as if Shoestring had grown very long in the legs. Old Jake explained.

"Standin' on a trunk."

"A trunk? Mercy. Whatcha gonna buy this mornin', Jake?"

"Same."

Old Jake moved off to pick out his supplies. From month to month, his bill of goods varied little: a sack of flour, a can of lard, canned goods, today a new whetstone for his whittling knife, and a bone for Shoestring. Basics. Nothing fancy.

"Five dollars, Jake."

He fished out his money and asked Eb for a pencil and paper. In a shaky hand, he wrote:

Trunk lost. Old Miller Road. Found. Come to Stillwaters Farm.

He handed it to Eb and asked him to post it on the bulletin board.

"What's in the trunk?" Eb asked.

"Don't know."

Old Jake met the morning regulars coming as he was going. "Set with us a spell, Jake," they offered.

"Can't. Got to get on."

The Stillwaters Farm, where Old Jake had directed the owner of the trunk, was in reality a hardscrabble patch of earth that had produced very little over the years besides rocks and trouble. In fact, Old Jake marked his years by the plagues that had visited him on it. There was the Year of the Crows, the Year of the Twisters, and the Year of the First Baptist Church of Quail's Good Samaritan Ladies' Committee. The good ladies of that committee had kind intentions in trying to get the old hermit to come to church, but each time they came they left behind the scent of teacakes and rose perfume, and Jake would grumble to Shoestring about it for days. In dark moments he muttered aloud to himself, wondering what plague planned to pay him a visit this year.

Old Jake quickly forgot the trunk. Shoved into a corner, it became a backrest for Shoestring, who through the winter months chose to curl up beside it rather than at the foot of Old Jake's bed. By spring, it had become a catchall and was covered over with dirty long johns and overalls. By first planting, no one had yet claimed the trunk.

With pumpkins beginning to sprout, Old Jake now needed Shoestring to sleep outside and keep rabbits from snacking on his crop. But Shoestring, for the first spring ever, whimpered each evening to return to the house.

"What's got into you, dog? Them rabbits're gonna go plumb wild with you in here."

But he let Shoestring in anyway, and the old hound happily curled up beside the trunk. By the third night of this, Jake had lost his patience. Shoestring was going to have to sleep outside, and it looked like the trunk was going to have to go with him.

Old Jake cleared it off and dragged it to the middle of the room. He had waited a proper time for someone to claim it, so it wouldn't be too unneighborly of him to open it now. He raised up the hammer and with a couple of hard knocks broke the lock. He lifted the lid slowly, almost reverently, like a young boy discovering a pirate's chest of gold. With lid up and contents revealed, Old Jake stumbled back as if he'd been slapped. For inside was no gold. Inside were skirts. Cotton calico skirts. He stepped up to the trunk again, reached down, and gingerly fingered one of them.

"Well I'll be, Shoestring," was all he could say, scratching his head at the same time. He scratched his head so long he finally scratched up an unpleasant thought. And it was this thought that made him slam the trunk shut, shove it back to the corner, and sit on it. A dark superstition had hatched inside of him. Perhaps in opening the trunk, he had set loose a host of mischievous spirits. He was, after all, a believer in plagues. For a fourth night Shoestring slept curled up against the trunk.

The next morning, a soft spring rain came. "As gentle as them skirts," he remarked to Shoestring, remembering how soft the calico cloth had felt beneath his rough hands.

By noon, the rain had turned wicked and wild. Puddles grew into rivers. Lightning bolts crashed to earth. And once again Old Jake, alone, battled it out with his plague. He was sure this would be the Year of the Storms.

Jake set out some buckets to catch the leaks and took up his whittling. No point in getting excited at the thought of his seedlings washing downstream. He knew when he was licked. "If she's gonna come, let her come, Shoestring." And he worked his knife on the wood to the beat of the bucket drops.

By nightfall the buckets had filled to overflowing. Old Jake couldn't empty them fast enough. Water began to pour in under the door. He feared that if he didn't stop this invasion, his cabin would wash downstream with his crop. He gathered all he had in the way of cloth and barricaded it against the crack under the door. But still the water came. When it began to swirl around the soles of his boots, his eyes lit upon the trunk.

He opened it up, bent down, and flung the skirts out one by one. He sent them flying in every direction, winging their way around the cabin like a flock of tropical birds. They landed on the floor and helped to drink up the water. And when the last skirt fluttered earthward, the rain stopped. Suddenly. As quickly as if someone had turned off a faucet. Old Jake, standing in water, stood still a moment and soaked up that silence. Then he set to work to clean up the mess.

Come daybreak, Old Jake was up to his elbows in soapsuds, bent over a washboard. He was scrubbing skirts. He'd used them to mop up the water and years of dirt gathered on his floor. His cabin had never looked cleaner, but the skirts were in sad shape.

"Besides," he confided to Shoestring, "they're kinda pretty, ain't they?" Old Jake felt superstitious about the skirts. After all, didn't the storm stop when he let them out? Shoestring didn't care about the skirts. He lay curled up on the porch in his new doghouse.

Skirts clean, Jake pinned them on a clothesline. It was the most color that Stillwaters Farm had seen since the Good Samaritan Ladies' Committee came with teacakes and Bibles the year before.

Skirts flapping in the breeze, Old Jake surveyed his soggy pumpkin field. All was lost, even the scarecrow. A few days of sunshine dried out the field and Jake began to replant his pumpkins.

The night after the last seed was planted, Old Jake put down his whittling knife and picked up scissors, needle, and thread. He was so happy about the storm shutting down, he felt almost silly. He even dressed his new scarecrow in a skirt and cut up another to give it a neckerchief. Then he made one for himself and one for Shoestring, too.

The next morning Old Sally's feedbag split open and her oats spilled all over the ground. No problem. One more skirt disappeared from the clothesline. Old Jake was beginning to become as handy with needle and thread as he was with a whittling knife.

No more wind whistling through the holes in his overalls. The skirts took care of that. No more sun beating down on Old Sally's head as she pulled the plow across the pumpkin field. The skirts took care of that. And no more hard porch for Jake as he took turns whittling and sewing in the evenings. The skirts took care of that, too. His place began to look downright merry. His spirits began to lift. And the days passed in sunshine and gentle rains. The pumpkin plants grew greener and fuller than ever, and it seemed that for this season at least, plagues would be held at bay.

Old Jake didn't even grumble much when he saw the First Baptist Church of Quail's Good Samaritan Ladies' Committee bumping up his road. He set down his whittling and stepped to the edge of the porch. The plump lady with the big smile and big roses on her dress led the procession. "Mornin', Mr. Jake," she almost sang, chipper as a song-bird. "Fine crop you have growin' there."

Old Jake felt a smile of pride creeping up to his lips. He coughed instead. The Good Samaritans, a bit nervous about being there, cleared their throats in response. A gentle chorus of *mmm, mmm*'s set up. Old Jake stood there and waited for other words.

The lady with the big smile and big roses on her dress noticed the three skirts flapping on the line. "Why, I must say. Your farm is positively pretty this spring. Is there a Mrs. Jake now?"

Old Jake didn't say.

The Good Samaritan continued, unruffled. "Well, we know you're busy with your farm and all, so we'll say our piece and leave you be. We've come to invite you to our church picnic by the river on Sunday. We'd be blessed to have you come. And, oh yes, we brought you these."

As Old Jake reached out to receive the teacakes, his fingertips brushed the soft white glove on her hand. "Much obliged," he muttered, feeling as awkward in his speech as a newborn calf on its legs. A soft breeze set up and the scent of rose perfume, heretofore swirling around the ladies, now settled into his whiskers. That sweetness, the teacakes, the company of kind folks, the sunshine, the day, the greenness of his good fortune—all, all for a moment unfolded in his heart as would a tender flower, and Old Jake revealed an answer that surprised himself and certainly stunned the Good Samaritans.

"I'll think on it."

The day the white pickup came rattling up his road, Old Jake had but one skirt left pinned to the clothesline. This last one he'd left out as a good luck symbol of sorts. He liked to look up from his whittling from time to time to watch it flap in the autumn breeze.

Old Jake stood with Shoestring beside him, absentmindedly scratching his faithful hound's head as the man and young, tow-headed girl climbed out of the truck. They approached the cabin, the girl following shyly behind the man. At one point the girl tugged at the man's coat, whispered something in his ear, and pointed to the skirt on the clothesline.

"Mornin'," the man said, his hat in his hand. "My name's Otis Brown and this here's my daughter, Sarah. We saw a sign in town said you found a trunk in the road some time back. Man named Sweeney told us we might find it here."

Old Jake followed their gaze to the trunk on the porch.

The man continued. "It was full of skirts. Them skirts belonged to my wife. We lost her this winter. I wanted to find the skirts if I could. For my daughter to have."

The little girl came out from behind her father now and stood beside him, holding his hand. She scuffed the toe of her shoe in the dirt. She sneaked a glance at the hermit, then dropped her gaze to the ground again.

It was Old Jake's turn to talk now, something he wasn't used to doing and didn't particularly like. What could he say? He'd used up all the skirts but one. He did manage, however, to put together more words in one stretch than he'd put together all that year. "It was me found the trunk. Mighty sorry 'bout that," he said, looking at it. Shoestring was curled up inside. "Didn't think no one was comin' for it. Used the skirts to help out around the place. Mighty sorry. Only got the one left," he said, turning toward the clothesline. Troubled by the girl's loss, and that he had nothing to give, he scratched his head hoping for a thought to tell him what to do. The young girl quietly came to stand beside him. It was a comfort to Old Jake. And thus for a time they stood together, alone with their own thoughts and the gentle breeze that caught at the skirt.

He went to the line, unpinned the skirt, and folded it in his hands. He walked back over, stooped his tall frame down, and held the skirt out in offering to the little girl. She quietly received it.

"Mighty sorry 'bout your mama," Jake said, his gravelly voice soft this once. "If you'll come inside, I got something I'd like to give you."

Old Jake pulled his only chair up to the chest of drawers, opened the top one, and lifted the little girl onto the chair. On tiptoes, she peeked over the edge of the drawer and saw a wonderful collection of wood carvings. "Take whichever one you want," he said.

The little girl beamed at Old Jake. He beamed back. She gently fished through the oldest carvings: the ones of dogs, and guns, and long-bearded men. And her fingers began to play with the newer ones: roses and doves and dolls. Finally, she picked. A painted carving. A doll wearing a calico skirt.

"I'd like this one, please."

Old Jake nodded, then lifted her off the chair.

That year Old Jake was blessed. He reaped a bountiful harvest. As it turned out, no plague visited him, and he remembered it as the Year of the Skirts. With each passing year, nature smiled upon him more, treated him more kindly. And he stored away memories of plagues, along with other unhappy memories.

Old Jake never saw the little girl again, but sometimes wondered about her. Wondered if she still had the doll and still liked it. How she was getting along without a mama or if by now she had another one.

And had the little girl paid Old Jake a visit in later days, she may not have found him holed up at Stillwaters Farm. She may instead have found him at Eb Sweeney's store, sitting among the circle of morning talkers. Not talking much, mind you, but listening and whittling.

Or she may even have spotted him, on a rare Sunday, sitting in the back pew of the First Baptist Church of Quail, his gravelly voice sending an occasional hymn to heaven.

C. Anne Scott began writing for children while living and teaching on the West Texas plains. It was there she encountered the inspiration for the character of Old Jake. Her work with street children in Fort Worth and her teaching days at Cal Farley's Boys Ranch in the Texas Panhandle moved her to write for children. Although she has published numerous newspaper and magazine articles, her preferred audience is children. A self-described "literary activist," she strongly believes that the power of the written word can open hearts and minds to greater understanding and awareness.

C. Anne Scott graduated summa cum laude from Texas Christian University, earning a bachelor's degree in English and history. *Old Jake's Skirts* is her first children's book and the fruit of a long-held dream. She hopes to make many more books for children. Presently she teaches, writes, and lives with her son Benjamin in a small Texas town.

David Slonim earned a bachelor of fine arts degree in illustration from Rhode Island School of Design in 1988. He creates artwork for a diverse range of clients, including advertising for IBM, UPS, and T.G.I. Fridays; book covers for Disney Press, Scholastic, and Pocket Books; magazine illustrations for *Reader's Digest, Money,* and *Sports Illustrated;* and character design for Tony's Frozen Pizza.

David lives in the Midwest with his wife—his high school sweetheart—and three sons. In his spare time, he enjoys fine art painting outdoors, long bike rides through the corn fields and pastures near his home, and writing stories, poems, and silly songs for his kids.